*For my grandfather
and my father,
who always loved T. R.,
and for Nicolas, Charles, and Justin,
who will come to love him too*

THE
ONE BAD THING
ABOUT FATHER

by F. N. Monjo
Pictures by Rocco Negri

🏛 HarperTrophy
A Division of HarperCollins*Publishers*

Grateful acknowledgment is made to the following for permission to use copyrighted
material:

Illustration by Theodore Roosevelt is reproduced with the permission of Charles
Scribner's Sons from *Crowded Hours*, page 96, by Alice Roosevelt Longworth.
Copyright 1933 Charles Scribner's Sons; renewal copyright © 1961 Alice Roosevelt
Longworth.

"Punkydoodle and Jollapin" from *Tirra Lirra* by Laura E. Richards. Copyright 1935
by Laura E. Richards. Reprinted with permission of Little, Brown and Company.

I Can Read Book is a registered trademark of HarperCollins Publishers.

Library of Congress Catalog Card Number: 71-85036
ISBN 0-06-024334-1 (lib. bdg.)
ISBN 0-06-444110-5 (pbk.)
First Harper Trophy edition, 1987

Contents

Chapter One

ARCHIE AND I

I'm Quentin.

Here's my brother Archie.

And here's Father.

There's just one bad thing about Father.

He's President of the United States.

That means he has to live in the White House.

And all the rest of us—
Mother
Alice
Ted

Kermit
Ethel
Archie
and me—

9

we all have to live there too.

There's one thing Archie and I
can't understand about Father.
I mean, Father could have been
a boxer or a wrestler.
He can even do jujitsu.

Mother says

he could have headed the police force

in New York City forever if he had wanted to.

Our brother Ted says
Father could have kept on being a cowboy
on his ranch in the West.
Father showed Archie and me his brand
for branding cattle. Here it is:

Father could have been a general.
Our sister Alice says
Father was a brave soldier and
helped win a war in Cuba.

And Father could have been a hunter.
Our brother Kermit says
Father knows how to catch
wildcats and bears.

Now if Father can do all these things,
what Archie and I would like to know is
how come he'd rather be President?

Being President can practically
ruin your whole life.
Presidents have to read lots of books.
They have to shake hands with congressmen.
They have to tell jokes to policemen.
They have to make lots of speeches.
They have to play tennis with senators.
They have to work out with prizefighters.
They have to go horseback riding
with cowboys.
And they have to have dinner
with lots of foreign princes.
Archie and I don't get to see
half enough of Father.

Father feels pretty bad about it too.

He lets us come to his office

every afternoon at four.

And for an hour or so

he does whatever we want him to do.

Sometimes

we take the hose

and flood the sandbox.

Father draws a map for us with his

umbrella and tells us all about the war.

He shows us where the Russians and
the Japanese are fighting each other.
Then we get our boats.
Archie is the Russian navy,
and I am the Japanese navy.
I always get to sink Archie's fleet
because the Japanese
are beating the Russians.
That's what Father says.
He's trying to get them to stop fighting.

Sometimes we visit
our blue parrot, Eli Yale.

Sometimes when Father rides his horse, Renown,
he lets Ethel and Archie and me
take turns riding our pony, Algonquin.

Algonquin has a soft nose.

Charlie Lee takes care of him.

Sometimes we visit our other pets.
We say hello to Jonathan, the rat,
to our white guinea pig, Dewey, Jr.,
to our hens, Baron Speckle and Fierce,
and to Josiah, the badger.
Father brought Josiah home from
one of his hunting trips.
Josiah likes milk and potatoes.

Sometimes we feed the dogs,

Cuba

and Skip

and Jack

and Sailor Boy.

And that's all the pets

we have—

except for the two kangaroo rats,

the turtle,

the flying squirrel,

and Tom Quartz, the kitten.

One time I gave Tom Quartz a bath

in the bathtub. He nearly drowned.

Chapter Two

GOVERNMENT PROPERTY

We like to have Father around.
But Mother says we have to let Father
have a few hours to himself every day
or he will never be able to run the country.

So Archie and I get this gang
of ours together.
Father calls us The White House Gang.
And we find stuff to do.

But when you live in the White House,
you have to be careful.
Things don't really *belong* to you.
Nearly everything is government property.

25

Suppose you are riding your express wagon
in the hall, having a race
with your dog, Skip.
Suppose the wagon turns over and
your hand goes through a picture.
It's Mrs. Benjamin Harrison,
wife of the twenty-third President.
And that picture is government property!

Nobody likes it when you slide downstairs
on tin trays either.

"By Godfrey!" says Father. "Don't you
bunnies know how dangerous that could be?
Suppose some senator got hurt?"

Suppose you and Archie and everybody
are having a stilt race on the lawn
and you happen to run
through a flower bed.

Here come the Secret Service men
and the White House police.
You have to get right out
of that flower bed.
It's government property too!

If Father catches you putting
spitballs on Andrew Jackson, he gets mad.
Andrew Jackson was the *seventh* President.
He's government property too!

Suppose you and your gang slide down
the awning over the front portico.
It's too steep to climb back up.
The police pull you back by a rope.
By Godfrey!
You can't play with awnings.
They're government property too.

29

You can't even visit your brother
when he's sick.
When Archie had the measles,
he was upstairs in his bedroom.
He hadn't seen Algonquin for weeks.
So I went to Charlie Lee, and we
sneaked Algonquin into the basement,
past the White House police.

We rang for the freight elevator.

Then we all got on.

Charlie and I had to *push* Algonquin.

31

We all went upstairs and
had a long visit with Archie.
It cheered him up a lot.
But the minute Father found out,
he sent Algonquin
right back to the stable.
"By Godfrey, Quentin! How can you be
such a muttonhead! It's preposterous!
You know perfectly well you can't
bring a pony into the White House
on the freight elevator!
It's *government property!*"

Chapter Three

AT OYSTER BAY

Archie and I have much more fun
in summer at our house on Oyster Bay.
Nothing is government property there.
Our big brothers, Ted and Kermit,
are home from school.
And sometimes our big sister, Alice,
is there too.
Alice usually helps Father run the country.

Alice isn't here this summer though.

Father says she's on a junket.

A junket is a trip to China and Japan.

Father likes to write letters to us.

Here's a picture Father drew

in a letter to Alice.

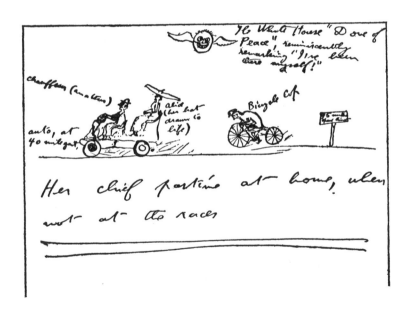

He drew the bicycle cop because
Alice loves to speed.
She races her car along
at twenty-five miles an hour!
Alice has her picture in the paper
practically every day.

Some man once asked Father why
he didn't do something about Alice.
Father said, "I can do one of two things.
I can be President of the United States.
Or I can control Alice.
I cannot possibly do both."

This summer, while Alice is away,
Archie and I are helping
Father run things.
This way we may get to see
more of Father.

If the Russians and the Japanese
would quit fighting,
Father would be pleased as punch.
And so would we.
Father sent a telegram to Russia,
asking them to stop fighting.

He sent another telegram to Japan,
asking them to stop fighting too.

Soon after that, a big ship came
to Oyster Bay.
Two Russians got off.
They wanted to see Father
about ending the war.

Archie and I were waiting
for them on the dock.
We pretended we were fishing.
But we were watching
every move they made.
And we reported their arrival to Father.

We knew some Japanese gentlemen were coming.
They wanted to talk to Father too
about ending the war.
Archie and I went to town.
We hung around and hitched
a ride home with them.
And then we reported their arrival
to Father.
The peace talks are coming along
quite nicely, thanks to Archie and me.

But Archie and Father and I
don't have to work *every* day
trying to end the war.
Sometimes we take a day off and play
Follow-the-Leader with Father.
Ethel and Cousin Lorraine
tag along too.
Here's how we go—
straight across the field,
into the duck pond and out again.
Father never goes around
anything that gets in his way.
We just go straight ahead.
Then we all hold hands
and run down the hill to the beach.
"How would you bunnies like a swim?"
says Father.
Father lets us go in with our clothes on.
He doesn't care.

Mother doesn't care either.

She's used to Father.

Other times, we put our bathing suits on
and go down to the float.

Archie brings Cousin Nick.

Ethel brings Cousin Lorraine.

And Mother and I come too.

We play a game called Stagecoach.

Here's how it goes.

Mother is the driver.

Father is the right front horse.

I'm the whip.

Archie is the guard.

Nick is the wildcat.

Ethel is the old lady passenger.

Lorraine is the left rear wheel.

Then Father starts telling this story,
and when he says your name,
you have to jump into the water.
And when he says "Stagecoach!"
just watch what happens.
"All right, everybody, here goes,"
says Father.
"We're traveling along at a fast clip.
The *driver* is cracking his *whip* . . .

when all at once the *old lady passenger* . . .
calls to the *guard.* . . .
She's seen a *wildcat*!" says Father.
"The *right front horse* rears up when he
sees the *wildcat* . . ." says Father.
"The *left rear wheel* is smashed. . . .
Then," hollers Father,
"over the cliff crashes the *STAGECOACH*!"
And when Father says "STAGECOACH!"
every one of us is in the water!

Sometimes Father goes camping overnight
with Ted and Kermit.
He fries chicken and potatoes,
and tells them ghost stories.
When Archie and I are bigger,
Father says we can go too.
Father tells us
about whippoorwills and owls and deer.
He knows where raccoons live.
He knows the songs of all the birds
and the names of all the flowers.

Chapter Four

THE END OF THE WAR

The Russians and the Japanese
came back again.
Father had lunch with them
and asked them to shake hands.
Then they sailed away to make peace.

51

Archie and I were in Father's study
when the telephone rang.
"What's that?" said Father.
Then he took us by the hand
and ran upstairs to Mother.
"Edie!" said Father. "They've made peace.
The war is over!"
"Theodore!" said Mother.
"What wonderful news!"
"A mighty good thing for Russia,"
said Father.
"A mighty good thing for Japan.
And a mighty good thing for us too!"

So all afternoon
Father and Archie and I
have been opening telegrams
from kings and emperors
and people all over the world.
They're all saying thank you to Father
for stopping the war.

Chapter Five

PUNKYDOODLE AND JOLLAPIN

Well, the war is over.

Summer is over too.

Ted and Kermit have gone back to school.

Mother and Ethel and Archie and I

are back in the White House with Father.

55

Mother says Father is planning to go
to Panama . . . to build a canal.

Archie and I are waiting for Father
to come in and play with us
before we go to sleep.
Sometimes he reads stories to us
from *Uncle Remus.*
Sometimes we play that he's the hunter
and we're the bears. Father tries
to paw us out from under our beds.

Sometimes he reads us a poem.

Here's a poem Father likes a lot.

PUNKYDOODLE AND JOLLAPIN

Oh, Pillykin, Willykin, Winky Wee,

How does the President take his tea?

He takes it in bed, he takes it in school,

He takes it in Congress against the rule.

He takes it with brandy and thinks it no sin.

Oh, Punkydoodle and Jollapin!

Then Father tosses me, Punkydoodle,
on top of Archie. Archie is Jollapin!
And he tickles both of us.
And then bang! Punkydoodle hits
Father with a pillow.
And plop! Jollapin hits him with another.
And a first-rate pillow fight begins.
Mother comes in, dressed for dinner.

"Theodore," she says, "we will be late
if we don't go down at once."
"Why, E-e-e-e-die," says Father,
"Punkydoodle, here, and Jollapin and I—"
"Theodore," says Mother, "you've rumpled
your shirt. You'll have to change it."
Then Mother and Father kiss us good-night
and turn out the lights.

Archie and I get under the covers
and talk about what we're
going to be when we grow up.

Archie says maybe he will be a general . . .
or a cowboy . . .
or a policeman . . .
But not me.
I've thought it over.
When I grow up, I'd like to be
just a plain man, with bunnies.
Like Father.

Author's Note

In one of his famous letters to his children, Theodore Roosevelt wrote: "I don't think that any family has ever enjoyed the White House more than we have. . . ." He was right, for he and his wife, Edith, and his children, Alice, Ted, Kermit, Ethel, Archie, and Quentin, had many wonderful times there. This story is written as Quentin might have told it as a child, but of course he never did so.

As the twenty-sixth President of the United States, America's beloved "T. R." lived in the White House from September, 1901, until March, 1909, spending his summers at Oyster Bay, Long Island, in the summer "White House," the home he named Sagamore Hill. It can still be visited today.

Theodore Roosevelt was one of our greatest Presidents. He gave us the Panama Canal and sent our fleet on its first goodwill tour around the world. And because he was able to help make peace between the Russians and the Japanese and avert the danger of a world war, he won the Nobel Peace Prize in 1906. Besides leading an active life in politics, he wrote more than a dozen books of history, biography, natural history, and memoirs.

But he was never too active or busy to play and joke with his children. This story, set in the spring and summer of 1905, suggests a few of the happy times the Roosevelt children had with their father.

Alice (Mrs. Nicholas Longworth), Ethel (Mrs. Richard Derby), and Archibald Roosevelt are still living. Theodore, Jr., and Kermit died fighting for their country in World War II. And, without ever having had children of his own, Quentin Roosevelt was killed at the age of twenty, on July 14, 1918, when his plane was shot down over enemy territory in France during World War I.